Just Grace and
the Terrible Tutu

Just Grace and the Terrible Tutu

Written and illustrated
by
Charise Mericle Harper

Houghton Mifflin Books for Children

Houghton Mifflin Harcourt
Boston New York 2010

Houghton Mifflin Books for Children is an imprint of
Houghton Mifflin Harcourt Publishing Company.

www.hmhbooks.com

The text of this book is set in Dante MT.
The illustrations are pen-and-ink drawings digitally colored in Photoshop.

Library of Congress Cataloging-in-Publication Data
Harper, Charise Mericle.
Just Grace and the Terrible Tutu / written and illustrated
by Charise Mericle Harper.
p. cm.
Summary: Eight-year-old Grace is excited to learn that her best
friend, Mimi, is going to become an older sister, but when both try
to be "mother's helpers" for a family renting a house on their street,
little Lily likes Grace best, causing Mimi to doubt herself and Grace
to form a plan to fix things.

ISBN 978-0-547-15224-0
[1. Interpersonal relations—Fiction. 2. Self-confidence—Fiction. 3. Best
friends—Fiction. 4. Friendship—Fiction. 5. Sisters—Fiction.] I. Title.
PZ7.H231323Juj 2011
[E]—dc22
2010006768

Manufactured in the United States of America
QFF 10 9 8 7 6 5 4 3 2 1
4500265471

A special thank-you to Leah and her mom!

WHAT I DIDN'T KNOW I DIDN'T KNOW

Best friends can be full of surprises. I already knew that, but sometimes even knowing something doesn't mean it still can't surprise you when it happens. That's why I was 100 percent surprised when Mimi said she had been keeping a secret from me and wanted me to read a special letter. Even though I had to go to the bathroom I sat right down with the letter. Some things can be more important than nature—plus I'm kind of an expert at holding it.

Dear New Sister,

I can hardly wait to meet you. I am so, so, so, so excited! Mom and Dad said I had to not tell anyone about you but my brain was about to explode so they finally said I could tell Grace. Yay! But she has to promise to not tell the world—which of course she can do, because she is a good secret keeper.

Grace is my best friend in the whole world, and guess what? She lives right next door, so when you get here you can see her every day just like I do. You have to call her Grace, though, and not Just Grace like they do at school. They only do that because when Miss Lois, our teacher, was naming the four Graces in the class, she got confused and named Grace that by accident.

Grace is great—for sure you are going to like her. Mom and Dad are pretty nice too. They sometimes have rules but I am sure you will get used to them and not mind so much. Mom is really good at reading bedtime stories and Dad is an expert swimmer. When you get old enough you can hold on to his back and he will dive up and down like a dolphin. It's really fun, but first you will have to know how to hold your breath and blow bubbles. You might have to get some lessons for that.

Mom said I get to pick out some fun stuff for your room. I can't wait to make it super cute for you.

There are some boys, Max and Sammy, that live near here too, but you don't have to play with them if you don't want to.

Lots of love,
Your new big sister,

Mimi
xoxoxoxo

P.S. The boys don't live in our house, but you might see them in the yard sometimes.

WHAT YOU MIGHT SAY IF YOU ARE SURPRISED OUT OF YOUR MIND

"Mimi! What? You're getting a sister! OMG. I can't believe it!" I had to whisper the OMG part because Dad says I'm not allowed to say that anymore. It's on his list of improper English-language words. I tried to complain to Mom, but she just said, "That's what happens when you have a dad who studied English in school. Plus it means he cares about you and how you sound." Maybe, but mostly I think he just likes making up rules.

I had a million and one questions for Mimi. Is your mom pregnant? How come she doesn't look fat? How do you know it's going to be a sister? When is she coming? Do you get to pick out her name? Can I help decorate the room? Wow! I flopped myself back on the bed and rested for a second. Not knowing stuff and being full of questions can really be tiring.

Mimi was excited to tell me everything. She said her mom wasn't fat because she wasn't pregnant. And instead of her mom getting pregnant and having a baby, her family was going to adopt one. The only thing she wasn't sure about was if the new sister was going to be a baby or one who could walk already. But whatever the sister was, Mimi said she was sure she would be little, sweet, and super cute. And she was 100 percent excited about it.

BRAIN IS ALREADY THINKING OF GOOD GIRL NAMES.

I got right to work thinking of some really good girl names, but Mimi said the little sister might come with a name already. Mimi's mom had already made some rules about the name. If the sister was two or three, they had to keep the name she came with. Mimi said they were only going to change it if the sister was still a baby.

"Wow, Mimi!" I had to say "wow" again, because stuff like a new sister does not happen very often in a life. "I know," said Mimi, and then while she waited lying on my bed, I ran to the bathroom.

WHAT IS HARD

Mimi said she could hardly wait to get her new sister, and that the waiting part was taking forever. "When do you get her?" I asked. "Can you go on Saturday?" Mostly my parents did shopping stuff and errands on Saturdays and Sundays. Once when we were getting a new kitchen table and chairs we even had to rent a trailer and stay overnight in a hotel. They were really far away, but Mom loved them, so Dad had to say yes.

Mimi said she didn't think it was that easy, because her mom and dad were still getting interviewed and tested to see if they would be good parents. Mimi said even though they were a great mom and dad to her, it wasn't good enough. "They still have to take a super-big test," said Mimi. "And write tons of e-mails, fill out lots of papers, and do lots of talking on the phone. Then at the end, after they pass, the tester people are going to come to our house and look at everything. And they'll probably even look in my room!"

Mimi seemed nervous about that, and she was right to be worried, because Mimi's room is a disaster. She has the messiest room I have ever seen. She was for sure going to have to clean it up. And just when I was thinking that, Mimi said, "I'm for sure going to have to clean up my room." It was like she could read my mind. Good friends are like that.

THOUGHTS MOVING FROM MIMI'S BRAIN TO MY BRAIN.

IT'S FOR SURE GOING TO TAKE MIMI FOREVER TO CLEAN HER ROOM.

THOUGHTS MOVING FROM MY BRAIN TO MIMI'S BRAIN.

IT'S GOING TO TAKE ME FOREVER TO CLEAN MY ROOM.

WHAT I DID NOT KNOW

After we had finished with all the new-sister stuff, I suddenly remembered the other part of Mimi's letter that I wanted to talk about. I really love dolphins, so of course I had to ask Mimi about her dad. "Can he really swim like a dolphin? You know—the up-and-down part? How about if you close your eyes—does it feel like you're riding on a real dolphin?" Mimi shook her head no but said, "It's still pretty cool. Plus you don't have to worry about sharks." "Good point," I said. I'd forgotten about sharks. Sharks can ruin everything.

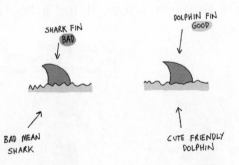

SHARK FIN
BAD

DOLPHIN FIN
GOOD

BAD MEAN
SHARK

CUTE FRIENDLY
DOLPHIN

The wrong fin can ruin your fun.

Before she went home for supper, Mimi made me promise not to tell her sister secret to anyone—not even Augustine Dupre. This was a hard promise to make. Augustine Dupre is the flight attendant who lives in the little apartment in my basement, and even though she is all grown up, she is still one of my best friends. One of the best things about Augustine Dupre is that she is a great listener. It's always super easy to tell her stuff. Sometimes I tell her things that I didn't even know my brain was thinking. The words just come out of my mouth and float straight up to her ears. I thought about it for a moment and

AUGUSTINE DUPRE'S EARS ARE SUPERPOWERFUL MAGNETS THAT PULL THE WORDS OUT OF MY MOUTH.

then I said, "Okay, I promise!" But inside my head my brain was thinking, *It's not going to be easy.*

WHAT MIMI RAN BACK TO TELL ME AFTER SHE LEFT

"Oh, I forgot," said Mimi. "You can tell your mom, because my mom told her so she already knows." So of course as soon as Mimi left again I ran into the kitchen to find Mom. "You knew? How come you didn't tell me? Mom! How could you keep such a super-big secret and not tell me?" Mom looked at me and said, "What secret, honey?" Mom is very sneaky. You can't fool her into telling you a secret just by pretending you already know it. "Mimi's sister secret!" I said. "Oh," said Mom.

"That secret. I'm glad she told you. Isn't it exciting? Now she'll be a big sister. She must be thrilled." Mom was so smiling and happy that I mostly forgot to be mad at her for keeping it from me.

FILLED WITH HAPPY
THOUGHTS AND
LOVE FOR MIMI

"And guess what, Mom?" I could hardly wait to tell her the next part. "She gets to pick out stuff for the room, and if it's a baby maybe even pick out her name. Isn't that cool? She could call her Vanilla or Jessica or

Violet or . . ." And then I sat down with some paper to make a list because I was super excited and my brain was thinking of all sorts of cool names. Sometimes great thoughts don't stay in your head. That's why it's good to write stuff down. It was a good thing I was doing that, because two minutes later Mom said, "Oh, I forgot to tell you about Mrs. Luther. Did you know she moved away for four months?" I was so surprised that if I hadn't already written down Jasmine, I would have for sure forgotten it. And that would have been too bad, because Jasmine is a really good girl name.

WHAT I SAID TO MOM

"Why are there so many surprises all of a sudden? Why can't there just be one new thing at a time? Why do we have to have a hundred new things and changes all on the same day?" Mom gave me her look that means *I don't know what you are talking about* and *Can you please calm down?* She uses the same look for two different things. After she does the look she always puts her hands on her hips.

Sometimes that part makes me smile because I am watching for it to happen, and then when it happens I think, *Ah-ha! I knew you were going to do that.*

"Okay, sorry. Sorry. Sorry. Where did Mrs. Luther go?" I tried extra hard not to use my attitude voice. If Mom even thinks I am using the attitude voice she gives me her big talk about attitude. And I didn't want to hear about appropriate voice choices—I wanted to hear about Mrs. Luther. It took Mom a long time to explain the Mrs. Luther story. She added a lot of details that I was not very interested in. Superlong stories can sometimes be tiring, and you might have to move around a lot while listening.

MRS. LUTHER'S STORY

Mrs. Luther, my neighbor, had left her house and gone to work at another school for four months. It was a teacher emergency thing. She was like a superhero substitute.

MRS. LUTHER, HAVE YOU GOT YOUR RUNNING SHOES ON? WE NEED YOU HERE AS SOON AS POSSIBLE.

HER BAGS ARE PACKED

←— RUNNING SHOES

This part of the story was not very exciting. Mrs. Luther is nice, but I was pretty sure I wasn't going to miss her very much while she was away. I do not go to her house or even see her very often. Mom was still talking, but I was having trouble listening because suddenly my brain was full of thinking about Crinkles. Crinkles is Mrs. Luther's cat, and just about the nicest cat in the whole world. Everyone that meets him just falls totally and madly in love with him.

I had to stop Mom's story right that minute, even though she was not finished talking. "Mom! What about Crinkles? Did she take him too?" I was asking this because the person who maybe loves Crinkles the most in the whole world lives right downstairs in my basement. If Mrs. Luther had taken Crinkles away, Augustine Dupre was for sure going to have a broken heart!

Of course Mom didn't know anything about Crinkles. She is not very good about collecting important information. Even though she loves to watch police shows, she would be a terrible detective.

WHAT MOM DID KNOW

While Mrs. Luther was gone, a French family that was friends with Augustine Dupre was going to move in. They were going to stay in Mrs. Luther's house so that they could be away from their own house while it was getting a new kitchen. This was the 100 percent exciting part of the story! Augustine Dupre is one of my most favorite people ever, and now we were going to get to live next door to some of her fancy French friends!

I lifted my arms up and said, "Mom, wow!" This is the new saying I made up for Mom. I only use it when she tells me something amazing, or when we are together and something super-good happens. It's special and just for her. She loves it!

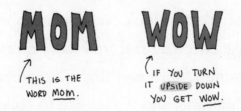

MOM

THIS IS THE WORD MOM.

WOW

IF YOU TURN IT UPSIDE DOWN YOU GET WOW.

Of course now I was dying to go downstairs and talk to Augustine Dupre. Usually I am not allowed to visit her after six p.m. or dinner, whichever comes first. Mom's big saying is "Grace, Augustine Dupre is not paying rent for the privilege of constantly entertaining a chatty eight-year-old." But this time even though it was after six-thirty, she did not say that. Instead she said, "Okay, go ahead." Maybe it was the power of the MOM, WOW.

AUGUSTINE DUPRE

Augustine Dupre has the best apartment ever. It is colorful and glamorous, and every time I see it, she has some kind of new French decoration making it look even fancier. She pretty much gets new stuff from France every week. Augustine Dupre is a flight attendant for a French airline, and if you like to collect nice stuff from France, this seems like the perfect job to have.

FANCY FRENCH
BOTTLES

FANCY FRENCH
TOWELS

FANCY FRENCH
FRAME

Augustine Dupre always knows when it's me knocking at her door. I made up a special knock so she wouldn't have to get worried and kick Crinkles out. So when I do my knock she always knows right away it's me.

Augustine Dupre is not allowed to have any pets in her apartment. This is one of Dad's rules, so if Dad is around, she has to shoo Crinkles away and pretend like he was never there.

As soon as I walked in I saw Crinkles sitting on Augustine Dupre's sofa. I couldn't believe Mrs. Luther had left him. It was like Augustine Dupre could read my mind, because the next thing she said was "I am going to help take care of Crinkles while Mrs. Luther is away." Then she put her fingers up to her mouth and made a shushing sound. I knew exactly what she was meaning. She was saying, "It's our secret—don't tell your dad." Of course she didn't have to worry about me, because I know how to keep a secret. And now I had two.

I like Crinkles, but lately I have been trying to be more careful about not touching him, so I sat in a chair instead of on the sofa. Mimi is so allergic to cats that even if I just pet Crinkles once, her nose will know about it and start sneezing as soon as I stand near her. Some friends are more important than cats.

WHAT AUGUSTINE DUPRE TOLD ME

Augustine Dupre is so smart. Without me even saying a word about it she knew exactly why I was visiting. She said, "I bet you want to hear about Mrs. Luther's house and my friends." She said her friends' names were Yvonne and Francois, and that they had a daughter name Lily. "I am sure you will like Lily," said Augustine Dupre. "She is very energetic. And she will absolutely love you. How could she not?"

Augustine Dupre gave my hand a little squeeze and then she told me something that was a complete surprise. "I was thinking you might like to help Yvonne by being a mother's helper. I have told her about you and she is interested. Would you like a little job?"

It was a MOM, WOW–OMG moment, but with Augustine Dupre I try to be more fancy, so I said, "Oh my gosh, that sounds great!" Being a mother's helper was not something I had ever been before, but you don't always have to be a doer to be a knower. And I was pretty much already knowing all about it.

WHAT YOU MIGHT THINK A MOTHER'S HELPER IS

If you had never heard about being a mother's helper before you would probably think it was a job where you help a mom do boring mom chores. Things like

washing clothes

cleaning the floor

putting things in cupboards

folding laundry

If you thought these things, then you would be wrong. This is not being a mother's helper. This is being a mom!

A mother's helper is a lot more fun, and that is because mother's helper is a person who plays with the kids and keeps them having fun. The mom likes this because then she doesn't have to listen to them, and she can do all her mom stuff without getting interrupted. Mother's helpers do things like play fun games with kids,

eat snacks with kids,

show kids how to make forts in the living room,

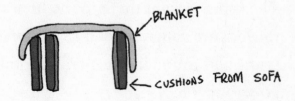

and keep kids away from the stove.

THE NUMBER ONE SURPRISING THING ABOUT BEING A MOTHER'S HELPER

You get paid real money to do it!

BEING A MOTHER'S HELPER IS EASY BECAUSE...

The mom is right there in the house in case the kids are naughty, get hurt, or forget to go to the bathroom. It's the perfect nothing-can-go-wrong job.

EXCUSE ME! JUSTIN'S PANTS ARE WET. IT COULD BE APPLE JUICE, BUT I'M NOT SURE.

I HAVE A PAPER TOWEL FOR YOU.

WHAT HAPPENED NEXT THAT WAS UNUSUAL

If I am visiting with Augustine Dupre and Mom wants me to come back upstairs, she usually yells down the stairs, but this time she came to the door instead. We had to shoo

Crinkles out of the apartment really fast. He was not happy.

Augustine Dupre and Mom talked about the new French neighbors, and Mom said she was looking forward to meeting Augustine Dupre's friends. I couldn't help myself—even though it wasn't polite, I had interrupt and tell Mom the exciting news. "Guess what, Mom? I'm going to have a job! I get to be a mother's helper." At first Mom seemed surprised, but then she asked a very good question. "Have you thought about asking Mimi to help you?" She was right. It was a great idea. The job would be a lot more fun if Mimi was going to do it too.

I gave Augustine Dupre a super-big hug when we left. I could hardly wait to meet the new people. They were going to be French, fancy, and fabulous!

THEY LOOK VERY FRENCH!

WHAT IS HARD TO DO IF YOUR BRAIN IS BUSY DOING LOTS OF THINKING

Go to sleep, but I made myself do it, because I couldn't wait until tomorrow to tell Mimi.

WHAT MIMI SAID AS SOON AS I TOLD HER ABOUT OUR NEW JOB

"Grace! This is the perfect way to practice being a big sister. It's just perfect!" And then Mimi gave me a big hug. She was so happy. If your best friend is super happy and smiling, it is really hard not to be that way too. We walked to school holding and swinging hands. It's too bad boys don't get to do that sort of thing, because it feels really nice.

When we got to school we saw Sammy and Max hiding behind one of the trees near the end of the playground. From where we were standing it didn't look like a very good hiding spot. At first we couldn't see why they were hiding, but then Mimi pointed to the swings and we saw Samantha Logan looking around. She is one of those girls who love to play chasing-boys games. Lucky for Sammy and Max, the lineup bell rang and Samantha ran off to find her class.

Mimi and I must have been smiling a lot, because while we were waiting to go in, Sammy and Max wanted to know what we were so happy about. I think maybe Max thought we had won a prize or something. When we told them we were excited about being mother's helpers for the new French family moving in to Mrs. Luther's house, both Max and Sammy said, "What?" at the exact same time. But I was pretty sure their *What?*s were meaning two very different things. Max's *What?* meant, That's it? That's why you're excited? I don't get it. And Sammy's *What?* meant, Mrs. Luther is gone? How can that be true?

HOW TO RUIN AN ENTIRE DAY OF SCHOOL FOR SAMMY STRINGER

Tell him that his favorite cool grownup friend has moved away. Mrs. Luther doesn't look cool on the outside, but inside she is about the only person who understands Sammy 100 percent of the time.

HOW TO MAKE SAMMY STRINGER FEEL A LITTLE BETTER AFTER SNACK TIME

Tell him that she will only be gone for four months, because you forgot to mention that part before.

WHAT ALWAYS GETS MISS LOIS A LITTLE GRUMPY

Miss Lois is our teacher, and she is slowly learning how to be more fun and interesting. Mr. Franks was our old student teacher and he came to our class to learn teacher stuff from Miss Lois, but I think she learned some stuff from him too. Especially how to not be boring and talk for too long when everyone has stopped listening. She hardly ever does that anymore, and pretty much everyone likes her much better now.

But there is one thing that changes the new fun Miss Lois back into the old non-fun Miss Lois in about two seconds. It happens so fast, it's like she's been zapped with super-grumpy power or something. And if you know our class, it's no big surprise that the zapper person is . . . Owen 1.

OWEN 1

HIS NAME BECAUSE THERE ARE LOTS OF OWENS IN OUR CLASS—NOT BECAUSE HE IS NUMBER ONE.

MY SHOES HAVE ZAPPING POWER.

Owen 1 sometimes thinks I am his friend, but mostly I am not, and this is a good thing because Owen 1 is almost always getting into trouble. His big number one troublemaking thing is his playing with his shoes. Normally this would not be a bad thing except for that Owen 1's shoes make a lot of noise. The noise-making part is the Velcro flaps. He pulls them apart and pushes them back together, and pulls them apart and pushes them back together, and pulls them apart and pushes them back together, over and over and over again. And each time he pulls them open, it makes a loud ripping, scratchy sound that pretty much bugs the whole class.

CLOSED
NO SOUND

FLIP OPEN
RIPPING SOUND

WHY IT'S A GOOD THING MISS LOIS IS NOT A CARTOON CHARACTER

If Miss Lois were a cartoon character her head would get big and smoke would come out of her ears, and then she would make a loud sound like a train whistle. That's how much she hates Owen 1 playing with his shoes.

Even though she tries real hard, Miss Lois can't be patient with Owen 1 forever. Every day she says the same thing: "Owen 1, will you please leave your shoes alone!" But after a while she just finally has to get mad. If she was allowed to, she would probably roll her eyes, but I don't think teachers can do that kind of thing. So instead she points to the door and says, "Owen 1, you get yourself down for a visit with Mr. Harris! Now!"

Mr. Harris is the principal of our whole school. And mostly he is not someone you want to visit in his office. I have a feeling that Owen 1 is probably going to have to change to lace-up shoes real soon.

CANNOT MAKE A SOUND.

MISS LOIS AND THE GIANT CLOUD OF BROWN

I am not a color expert, but I bet if grumpiness were a color it would be that brown blah color you get every time you mix all your paints together in a big mushy mess. That's the kind of color no one would ever make or choose on purpose. Even though I couldn't see it, I bet that was the color of Miss Lois's grumpy cloud. It stayed up over her head all through reading, math, and spelling, and right up until lunchtime. Miss Lois tried to make her words sound happy and normal, but we could all tell the cloud was still there. The cloud made everyone not like Owen 1 even more than they had not liked him before. This was too bad, because Owen 1 did not have a whole lot of extra liking energy to lose. I was glad I was not him.

HOW MIMI SURPRISED ME AGAIN

After lunch we get to have recess and go outside. Mimi and I hardly ever go over and hang out by the fake rock wall, but today Mimi wanted to go there. I was thinking that maybe she wanted to try climbing it, but mostly she just wanted to stay around where Marta and Olivia were playing with some of the other Fairy Girls. They call themselves Fairy Girls because their favorite thing to do in the whole world is to play princess fairy. Since we were standing there and Mimi was not talking, we ended up mostly listening to them play their game.

It didn't sound very fun. There was a lot of arguing about super fairy powers. "Princess Petaluna can totally fly into the cave and get the magic stone!" said Olivia. "No she can't!" shouted Marta. "She lost her wings!

Don't you remember? She has to go back and ask the Violet fairy to let her have some new ones! You always want to do what you want to do. It's not fair! If my fairy has to lose her wings, then yours does too!" Marta was really mad—she was shaking her arms, and both her hands were in fist shapes. Everyone was watching. We couldn't help it.

INVISIBLE WINGS

UNFRIENDLY FAIRY GIRL

At first Olivia looked like she might yell back at Marta, but then instead she said, "Fine! Princess Petaluna will walk into the cave! Now are you happy?" Olivia walked under the slide and pretended to pick something up from the ground.

We didn't get to see what was going to happen next because the bell rang and we had to go in. While we were running to line up, Marta ran over and said, "Do you want to play next time? It's really fun!" *NO way, thank you!* was what my brain screaming inside my head. But before my mouth could find a nicer way to say it Mimi said, "Okay, sure." And that is how she surprised me all over again.

WHAT I WAS WONDERING ABOUT

Mimi was not being her regular Mimi self. Fairy princess was not something she would normally want to play. I tried to ask her about it when we first sat down, but Miss Lois surprised us all by saying that today was going to be our first day of cursive writing. This was not something I was expecting, and for once it was something I wanted to learn, so I stopped not paying attention. All the girls in the class were excited—we could hardly wait to write in cursive. I don't think boys care so much about fancy writing. They never practice fancy letters like girls do.

Mimi and I have been practicing our names since last year. I already know how to make the big G and the big S all swirly and fancy. My name looks fantastic in script. I am glad that my name is not Valerie Newcome—she is not so lucky.

VERY
SWIRLY

MY NAME
LOOKS
FANCY → *Grace Stewart*

BOTH OF THESE
HAVE THE SAME
BOTTOMS.

NO FANCY
SWIRLS

Valerie Newcome

NOW NICE
POINTY V
HAS TO LOOK
LIKE A U

MISS LOIS IS VERY FAIR

Miss Lois said that everyone had to learn how to write all the letters in the whole alphabet, even the ones that were not in our names. Some people in the class were thinking the only reason to learn cursive was so that they could know how to sign their names fancy. They were not so excited about learning all the letters.

Sandra Orr put her hand up and said that she knew exactly why the girls should learn all the letters. Miss Lois is always really patient with Sandra, even though she knows that the words that come out of Sandra's mouth will probably not make any sense. Mostly this is because Sandra does not pay very good attention. Miss Lois's most favorite thing to say to her is, "Sandra, please try to keep your head out of the clouds." Sandra is an expert day-dreamer.

Sandra said, "When girls get married they sometimes get a new last name, so it's probably good to be ready by knowing all the letters before that happens." Miss Lois smiled and said, "Thank you, Sandra—that may be true, but there are many other reasons to learn cursive that are useful for both boys and girls." I bet the boys were not so happy to hear that. For sure Sammy was not happy, because he crossed his arms and flopped his head down. Learning cursive was not making him feel happier about Mrs. Luther leaving. I bet if I had the superpower of hearing thoughts, his brain would be saying something very grumpy.

WHAT OWEN 1 SAID

Miss Lois said one of the very helpful things about cursive was that it was a faster way to write down words than printing. She said the brain could think of words very fast, but a lot of the time it was hard for the fingers to keep up. As soon as she said this, Owen 1 started waving his hand around to ask a question. He was back in class and trying really hard not to play with his shoes. I saw him touching them, but he did not pull on the Velcro.

Finally Miss Lois pointed at him. She was probably expecting him to ask to go to the bathroom. That was one of his regular questions, but instead he wanted to talk about cursive writing. This was something of a surprise.

Owen 1 said that he had rocket-fast fingers when he played video games, but when he picked up a pencil to write they worked more like crummy old roller skates. I thought he was going to get in trouble for being so negative, but Miss Lois got really excited. She said that Owen 1 had used a wonderful analogy to explain how he felt. Of course Owen 1 was instantly proud even though nobody, and for sure not even him, knew what Miss Lois was talking about. Miss Lois loves to teach new stuff, so right away she explained what an analogy was.

An analogy is an example of one thing that you can use to help you explain another thing.

ROCKET SHIP GOES FAST

WE'RE FAST

WE LOVE VIDEO GAMES.

CRUMMY OLD ROLLER SKATES DON'T GO VERY FAST

WE'RE SLOW

WE DON'T LIKE TO PRINT.

Once she told us about it, I instantly knew that I had already been using analogies for a long time, even though I didn't know I was using them. It's nice to find out you are smarter than you thought you were. Thank you, Miss Lois!

ONE OF MY ANALOGIES

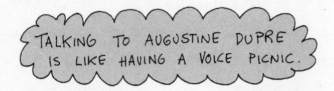

TALKING TO AUGUSTINE DUPRE IS LIKE HAVING A VOICE PICNIC.

WALKING HOME

Sammy and Max walked home with us. Max wanted us to all hang out in his front yard, but Mimi said we couldn't because we had to go inside and work at her house. I didn't know what work she was talking about, but it was a good thing we weren't going to be with Sammy, because Sammy and Mimi were thinking two very different things about Mrs. Luther leaving.

As soon as we got inside Mimi ran upstairs to the old filled-with-junk room that is next to her bedroom. This was the room that was going to be changed from the junk room into the new sister's room.

FOUR THINGS I WAS SURPRISED ABOUT

1. The old filled-with-junk room was now completely empty.

2. Mimi's room next door was picked up and clean.

3. I was not as excited about those first two surprising things as I would normally be.

This was because my stomach was growling with hunger.

I usually like to have a snack after school, so it did not help that Mimi's whole entire house smelled like yummy fresh-baked banana bread.

Mimi seemed a little disappointed when I asked if we could think of new sister room ideas in the kitchen near the banana bread instead of on the floor in the empty junk room. She had set up a bunch of papers and markers on the floor for us, so I knew she was disappointed that I was changing her plan. If my stomach is hungry it just doesn't matter what my brain is saying. My stomach pretty much always has to win.

Mimi's brain was stronger than her stomach, because she only ate one piece of bread and normally she could eat about five. Today I had three. Sometimes Mimi's mom has to guard the bread so we don't eat too much and ruin our dinner. But today she didn't even say one thing about it. She just smiled, hugged Mimi, and said, "Mimi is so happy that you are going to help her decorate her new sister's room." "You bet I am!" said Mimi. "And it's going to be pink!" That last thing Mimi said was my number four of surprises.

MIMI IS NOT BEING MIMI

It's important to be patient with your friends, no matter what. This is an important rule of friendship.

Sometimes a friend can surprise you and it's exciting.

Sometimes a friend can surprise you and it's not so exciting.

And then other times they can surprise you and you think, "Where has my friend gone? This person who looks like my friend is not acting anything like the friend that is my best friend." That is what I was thinking about Mimi, because Mimi and I have never been girls who love pink!

"All little girls love pink," said Mimi. This was not true, because a long time ago when Mimi and I were little girls we didn't love pink. When we were little my favorite color was orange and hers was yellow. But it sounded like Mimi had forgotten about that.

"Pink sounds lovely!" said Mimi's mom, and then they both looked over at me and smiled. I could tell they were waiting for me to say something nice. "Pink is girly," I said. It was the only thing I could think of that was true and that did not sound negative. "Exactly!" said Mimi. "And we have to be girly."

WHAT YOU DO WHEN YOU GET HOME FROM A CONFUSING VISIT WITH YOUR BEST FRIEND WHO MIGHT NOT REALLY BE YOUR BEST FRIEND BECAUSE MAYBE SHE WAS TAKEN AWAY BY ALIENS AND REPLACED WITH A ROBOT WHO LOOKS JUST LIKE HER

Write a new Not So Super comic, because drawing comics always makes me feel better about stuff.

WHAT WAS A SURPRISE AT BREAKFAST

Today was not a school day. Right away that makes everything about the day a lot better. I don't have to rush around getting ready, and I can hang out in my room and relax. That's why I was surprised when Mom said, "Grace. Breakfast. Now." Usually I only hear those words from Monday to Friday. I went downstairs in my pajamas and was just getting ready to complain when I saw Augustine Dupre standing in my kitchen. One hand was holding a bag from the doughnut store, and the other one was holding on to a little girl wearing a bright pink tutu.

"Oh, I'm sorry—were you still sleeping?" asked Augustine Dupre. She put her hand up near her mouth like she was worried. "We can come back later." I was surprised to see her there, but I did not want her to leave. "No,

I'm awake. See." And I jumped up and down a few times to prove it. "I'll get dressed. I'll be right back. Wait for me." And then before anyone could say anything else I ran upstairs to change. How embarrassing! Mom could have told me we had visitors! And I wasn't even wearing good pajamas. Ugh! Sometimes she drives me crazy.

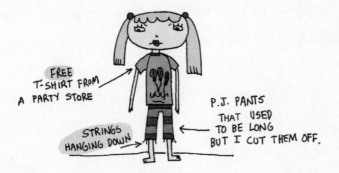

FREE T-SHIRT FROM A PARTY STORE

P.J. PANTS THAT USED TO BE LONG BUT I CUT THEM OFF.

STRINGS HANGING DOWN

WHAT YOU SHOULD DO IF YOU RUN OFF WHILE SOMEONE IS WAITING TO MEET YOU

Apologize. A lot!

WHAT HAPPENED NEXT

Mom said, "I'm sorry." I said, "I'm sorry." Mom gave me a look that meant, *How could you run off like that?* I gave her a look that meant, *You could have told me we had visitors.* And then a little voice interrupted everything and said, "Why is your shirt on backwards?" When something unexpected happens right in the middle of something serious, two things can happen.

1. You can get upset and maybe even cry.
2. You can laugh.

Sometimes you can't tell which of these two things your body is going to decide to do until the very second that it happens. Lucky for me I laughed.

WHAT LILY WAS LIKE

1. Lily was wearing a pink tutu.

2. Lily liked jelly doughnuts, but mostly she liked the jelly. She sucked the middle out of about twelve jelly doughnuts and left the empty little doughnut shells all over the table and floor.

DOUGHNUT LEFTOVERS

3. Lily wanted to play house. I had to be the baby.

4. Lily wanted to catch frogs. I was supposed to kiss them.

5. Lily wanted to play mermaid. I was the dry mermaid on land.

6. Lily wanted to play doggy. I was the doggy.

7. Lily was a lot of work.

WHAT I WAS KNOWING ALL OF A SUDDEN (PART ONE)

Being a mother's helper was not going to be as easy as I thought it was.

WHAT I WAS KNOWING ALL OF A SUDDEN (PART TWO)

This job was maybe going to be more perfect for Mimi than it was for me.

WHAT WAS GOOD

After a while, which seemed like forever, Augustine Dupre finally said it was time for them to go. I thought that maybe four hours had passed, but when I looked at the clock it had only been one hour and twenty minutes. I don't know why it really seemed a whole lot longer. Augustine Dupre said they would come back later so I could meet Lily's mom.

"Maybe you could help her tomorrow," said Augustine Dupre. "It's moving day, so I'm sure she will need you." "Yay," said Lily. "Can I stay here until tomorrow?" Lily did not want to leave. "She likes you," whispered Augustine Dupre. This sounded like a good thing, but at the same time part of me was not so 100 percent sure.

Lily finally stopped crying when Augustine Dupre promised they would come back in the afternoon. *"Au revoir,* Grace," said Lily, waving. It was the first French thing she had said.

After they left I could tell that Mom was in love with Lily.

"Isn't she just the cutest thing? Little girls are so sweet. I bet playing with Lily makes you excited about Mimi's new sister. You're going to have so much fun with her," said Mom. She smiled and looked at me. I nodded my head but didn't say anything. I wasn't sure my brain believed her.

WHAT I WAS WORRIED ABOUT ALL OF A SUDDEN

I had never thought of it before, but now all I could think of was one big scary question.

What if Mimi's new sister was just like Lily? A sister like that could change everything.

WHAT MIMI CANNOT WAIT TO DO

Mimi was disappointed that I had already seen Lily. She said she could hardly wait to get started on our new job. I tried to tell her that it was probably not going to be as easy as she thought it was, but she said she didn't care. She spent all morning looking out the window and walking around in the front yard hoping to see Lily.

While we ate lunch I tried to tell her about all the games Lily wanted to play, and how playing with a four-year-old was really tiring and hard, and not at all easy like I thought it was going to be. Mimi looked at me like I was crazy. "Mimi, you have to believe me. Just wait—you'll see." I kept trying to warn her, but it was too late. Augustine Dupre and Lily were already coming up the sidewalk.

HOW TO INTRODUCE YOUR BEST FRIEND IF YOU WANT A FOUR-YEAR-OLD TO LOVE HER

"*Bonjour,* Grace!" Lily ran up and hugged me before I could do or say anything. It was nice. I felt a little like Crinkles must feel every time Augustine Dupre sees him. Mimi was just standing there, so I unwrapped Lily's arms from my middle and introduced her to Mimi. "Lily, this is my best friend in the whole world.

Her name is Mimi. Mimi loves to play all sorts of girl games. She is really fun." Mimi said, "Hi, Lily. I'm so happy to meet you." But Lily just ignored her and hid behind my legs.

Augustine Dupre made Lily say hi to Mimi. It was a very small hi and it was in English. I think Mimi was disappointed.

THINGS YOU CAN TRY TO DO TO MAKE A FOUR-YEAR-OLD LIKE YOU

1. Make a silly hat out of paper.

←—PAPER HAT

2. Set up a game of knock down the stuffed animals.

←— STUFFED ANIMALS WAITING TO BE KNOCKED DOWN WITH THE BALL.

←— THE BALL

3. Offer up a really long piggyback ride.

I SURE WISH I COULD GIVE SOMEONE A PIGGYBACK RIDE.

4. Have real costumes out and ready to play fairy princess.

← PRINCESS COSTUMES

Mimi tried everything, but nothing was working to make Lily want to be with her. I tried to be super boring and was sitting with a magazine so Mimi could try to get Lily interested in her, but Lily just said, "No, thank you. I want to look at the magazine with Grace."

Poor Mimi. I couldn't tell exactly what she

was thinking, but I knew it was not happy thoughts.

CAN YOU SAY NO TO A FOUR-YEAR-OLD?

When Mimi went to the bathroom Lily said, "Let's play unicorn princess. You can be the unicorn and I am the princess." "That's so cute!" said Mom. She was totally listening in. "No, thanks," I said. "I don't feel like it." I did not want to be a unicorn. A unicorn is a horse with a horn. Horses carry people around, and I just knew that in about two seconds the princess would definitely be wanting to jump on the unicorn's back for a big long ride. I looked over at Mom. She was frowning with her hands on her hips. This was not a good sign. I knew that look. It was the beginning of her *You're about to get into trouble* look. It was a look I needed to make go away, fast!

"Okay, Lily—I changed my mind. I'll be a unicorn." Lily was filled with joy. In about two seconds she had even made me a costume. And that is how Mimi found me when she came back. I was Pinky Twinkle the galloping unicorn.

FASTER, PINKY TWINKLE! FASTER!

PAPER TOWEL TUBE TAPED TO MY HEAD (UNICORN HORN)

You cannot say no to a four-year-old. At least not when your mom is standing right there.

WHAT IS NOT FAIR

It is not fair to be getting into trouble for being Pinky Twinkle when I never wanted to be Pinky Twinkle in the first place. Mimi said, "You waited until I had to go to the bathroom, and then you took her away from me with your being a super-fun unicorn!" I tried to tell her I didn't want to be a unicorn, that she could be Pinky Twinkle, and that being a unicorn was not so super fun, but she didn't listen.

Of course Lily could hear us fighting, because even though I didn't want her to be, she was still on my back. Suddenly she started squishing my ribs with her legs and bouncing up and down. "I know, I know!" squealed

Lily. She pointed at Mimi and said, "You can be the evil troll!"

Mimi looked over and gave me a look I had never seen her do before. It was mean, scary, and frightening. It was the kind of look that stops heartbeats and gives shivers. It only lasted a second, but both Lily and I saw it. Then Mimi turned around and walked right out the door without saying a word.

MIMI
LOOK

"She did a real good troll face," said Lily. "She was scary." "Yeah, she was," I said. And because Mom was not around anymore I said, "Let's play something else."

Finally it was time for us to walk over to Mrs. Luther's house to meet Lily's mom. She was getting Mrs. Luther's house ready for the big move-in. Now I was suddenly not looking forward to the job anymore, and there was not even one idea in my head about how to solve the new Mimi-mad-at-me problem. Augustine Dupre said she and Lily would walk over first, and Mimi and I could come over when we were ready.

Augustine Dupre was smart. She knew I was having a problem. I was wishing she could be super smart and magic and know how to fix it, but that kind of thing only happens in movies—a twirl of the finger and then everything is okay.

WHAT LILY WAS NOT

Lily was not fabulous or fancy like I thought she was going to be. In one day she had almost gotten me in trouble with Mom and had made Mimi mad at me.

Now I was wondering if French kids started out just like regular normal kids and the fancy-fabulous part was maybe something they learned later on.

WHAT HAPPENED NEXT

I decided to stand around outside in my front yard while I tried to think of what to do. I did not want to go to Mimi's front door and have her yell at me. I was hoping that maybe she'd notice me and come outside to talk—somehow that seemed easier.

It was a good plan for getting noticed. First Crinkles saw me, and then Lily almost saw me. I did not want to go over to Mrs. Luther's house yet, not without Mimi. I needed more time. Luckily Lily didn't see me, and that was because I hid behind the big tree in the front yard before she could look over.

ME HIDING

The only person that actually saw me was Sammy. He was holding a big glass jar full of white things, like cotton balls but smoother. "Are you hiding from the cat?" He saw me peeking around the tree and Crinkles sitting at the other end of the yard. Sammy does not like cats, so this was a normal kind of question from him. "Shhh," I said. "Don't talk so loud. Whisper."

Of course now Sammy was full of questions. "Are you hiding from that lady over there?" He pointed to a lady who was holding Lily's hand—it was probably Lily's mom, Yvonne. "No, stop pointing! They'll see you." Sammy was not good at being sneaky. "The little girl," I whispered. "I don't want Lily to see me." Sammy started to laugh. "The little girl? You're scared of her?"

I had to do something fast or Sammy was totally going to ruin everything with his loud laughing. Lily would hear him, look over, and then be running over to make me carry her all over the yard again. When you want someone to stop what they are doing, it is sometimes a good idea to try to change the subject really fast.

THINGS MY BRAIN WAS THINKING IT COULD DO (NOT ALL GOOD CHOICES)

1. Kick Sammy in the leg.
2. Pretend-faint.
3. Climb tree.

4. Grab the jar from Sammy's hand.

5. Start dancing.

6. Handstand.

The handstand would have been good except that I don't know how to do one. I have tried and tried but I just can't hold myself up. For sure Sammy would have forgotten all about Lily if I was suddenly doing an excellent handstand right in front of him, but Lily might have seen that too. A good handstand is pretty noticeable.

WHAT MY BRAIN PICKED

I grabbed the jar out of Sammy's hands and said, "What's this?" It was a good choice because Sammy forgot all about Lily in about a second. "Hey, that's mine. Don't break it. It's a present from Mrs. Luther. She left it for me." At first I thought it might be something totally disgusting. Mrs. Luther once let Sammy borrow a jar of lion poop, so disgusting things were not surprising for them.

SAMMY'S JAR FILLED WITH WHITE ROCKS

"It's rocks," said Sammy. "Each rock is from a different place. And on the bottom of each rock is the name of the place where Mrs. Luther found it. Isn't that cool?" Sammy is the kind of boy who loves collections. This was a perfect present for him. All the rocks looked the same to me. They were small, round, and white. Sammy said he had a favorite, and it was from a place called Squamish in Canada. That sounded like a made-up name, but I didn't want to argue with him, so I didn't say anything about it not being real. I gave him back the jar so he could find his favorite and show me.

For sure Sammy was going to miss Mrs. Luther. I felt a little sad for him. Not that many people in the world understand Sammy as perfectly as she does. I'm pretty sure she is the only person in the world who was truly happy, and not only pretending to be happy, when Sammy said she could borrow his summer art project for a few months and hang it up in her house.

THIS IS WHAT SAMMY SAID AT THE BEGINNING OF THE SUMMER

"Every time I see the ice cream truck I'm going to try something different."

THESE ARE ALL THE DIFFERENT TYPES OF ICE CREAM

THIS IS WHAT SAMMY MADE AT THE END OF THE SUMMER

SUMMER ICE CREAM

WRAPPER FROM ICE CREAM TREAT

NOTE ABOUT IF HE LIKED IT OR NOT AND WHY

THICK BOARD FOR POSTERS

Mrs. Luther loved it, and she really did borrow it and hang it up in her kitchen for two whole months. Sammy said he might give it back to her for keeps when she gets back from her trip. Partly because she really loves it, and partly because his mom says it's taking up too much space in his room.

WHAT SAMMY SAID NEXT

"Okay, you don't have to hide anymore. She's gone." He said it without smiling, without laughing, and without making fun. My brain said, *Thank you, Sammy. You really are a nice boy.* My mouth said, "If I find any cool white rocks I'll save them for you." He seemed happy with that.

WHAT HAPPENED NEXT

I saw Mimi coming out of her garage with a bunch of stuff. "Should we take jump ropes?"

she shouted. She did not look one bit mad or unhappy, which was a big surprise. Even if my leg had been broken I would have said, "Yes, we must skip," because more than anything, I wanted us to be friends again and for Mimi not to be mad at me.

"Lily might like to play with this stuff," said Mimi. "Should we ask her mom if she wants it?" I was surprised and shocked and couldn't believe my ears, but I said, "Sure! Good idea." Mimi was amazingly still liking Lily.

LILY'S MOM

A few minutes later Mimi and I were standing on Mrs. Luther's porch. It was nice to have Mimi with me. On the way there I made myself a big promise, no matter what, this time I was not going to be a dolphin, a unicorn, a turtle, or any other kind of creature that could give a ride on its back. Sometimes you just have to make rules! Even if it makes you sound like a mom.

NO, I'M SORRY. RIDES ON THE BACK ARE NOT ALLOWED.

WHAT FEELS GOOD

Five minutes after we met Yvonne, who was very nice, the biggest part of me that was feeling good was my stomach. Lily's mom is a fantastic cook. We sat on Mrs. Luther's porch and ate fresh muffins and homemade strawberry and apricot jams. It was super tasty. Even Lily was not so much of a bother. I guess it's hard to be pesky when your mouth is full of food. I'm going to have to remember that. Mimi tried to sit next to her and talk, but

Lily was being shy and mostly wanted to sit in her mom's lap. From far away, she actually looked kind of cute, but that was probably because she was sitting on someone else that wasn't me.

THE PLAN FOR SUNDAY

Lily's family is moving into Mrs. Luther's house tomorrow at lunchtime. Mrs. Luther is letting them use all her furniture and kitchen stuff, so mostly they only have to move in their clothes. Yvonne asked us if we could watch Lily from eleven-thirty until two p.m. Of course we said yes.

Mimi was much more chatty than I was. She was totally organized and ready. If there was a mother's helper crown she would have been the one wearing it. She showed Yvonne a list of games, crafts, and fun activities that she had written down. Yvonne was very impressed. I was very impressed too, but secretly I was most glad that there wasn't one single unicorn thing on the whole list.

WHAT I WAS HAPPY ABOUT

After the little meeting Mimi and I went back to her house. That was a huge relief. I was glad not to be staying at Mrs. Luther's and playing with Lily for the rest of the afternoon. Mimi and I did not talk about the morning and how Lily had wanted her to be a troll. I was glad about that too. Sometimes if things are happy and good, it's not the best idea to talk about something sad and upsetting.

Mimi really wanted us to work on her new sister's room, so I tried to help and keep everything smiley. Even though it was going to be pink and frilly, which is not so much my style, I still wanted to be filled with energy about it.

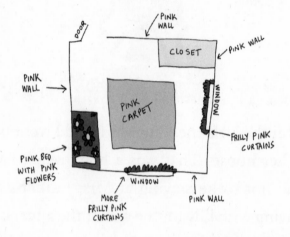

THE BEST PART OF THE NEW ROOM

While we were drawing what the room was going to look like Mimi's dad came in to see how it was going. When he saw the plan he said, "Wow. That's a lot of pink." That's exactly what I was thinking too, but I had not said it out loud. "I'm not sure all that pink is going to look good," said Mimi's dad. "What if you just make one of the walls pink?" "Oh, Daddy! This is a girl's room! Girls love pink!" Mimi was getting upset.

Mimi's dad tried to get her to be calm. "Mimi, you're a girl. Your room isn't all pink." But Mimi wasn't wanting to change her mind. "Daddy, that's because I'm not little. Little girls like dolls, and princesses, and pink! It's a fact!"

Mimi's dad was not giving up. He said, "Mimi, that's silly. You never loved pink or even dolls when you were a little girl. Remember? Listen, if you tone down this room and have just one wall of pink, I'll make you a deal. I'll let you paint it yourself. Think about it. Okay?" Mimi was beaten. "Okay, Daddy," she said. She sounded sad and unhappy, but as soon as her dad was gone, she jumped up and down and said, "Grace! Did you hear that? We get to paint the room ourselves!" I was pretty excited about that too. Not all parents let you paint a room all by yourself.

WHAT I DID AS SOON AS I GOT HOME

After dinner I went upstairs to draw a new Not So Super comic. I wasn't in a bad, sad, or even unhappy mood, which is when I usually draw them. This time I just had a really funny idea.

That night before bed I flicked my lights on and off for Mimi. She did it to me too.

This is our good-night signal, and it was nice to have everything feeling regular and happy again.

WHAT I HAD FOR BREAKFAST

I have a little bit of a superpower. It's called empathy. Having empathy power means I can 100 percent tell when someone is sad, even if they are acting and pretending to be happy. When this happens I always use my energy to try to find a way to make them feel better. Usually when I feel my empathy power working I like to eat French toast. It's kind of like my superhero breakfast.

FRENCH TOAST AND SYRUP

This morning was different though because I was not feeling anyone's sadness. Instead, I was feeling like maybe I was going to be needing the extra energy for me. And that was mostly because I was worried about Lily. I was even wearing my good luck Super Girl underwear. Sometimes it's a good idea to be as ready as possible, just in case.

SUPER GIRL UNDERWEAR

WHAT WAS SURPRISING ABOUT MIMI

I was just finishing off my breakfast when Mimi walked in. She was looking like I had never seen her look before. Normally Mimi and I do not wear pink, but today we were both being different. Me a little, Mimi a lot! My Super Girl underwear had a little bit of pink writing on it, but Mimi was an explosion of pink. I had hardly even ever seen pink-lovers wear so much pink. Sometimes if you are super surprised it's hard to think of what to say. And even if you don't mean to, you might just look at the person who is surprising you with your mouth open.

I was glad Mom walked in the room, because I was still being quiet. "Mimi, aren't we cheerful today," said Mom. "And what's that you have there?" Mom was pointing to a bag that Mimi was carrying. I hadn't even noticed it, mostly because I was so surprised about the pink. "It's balloons," said Mimi. "I've been practicing balloon animals." "Balloon animals? Wow, Mimi—that's so cool." I was glad to have something I could talk about. "What can you make?" "Not so much yet," said Mimi. "It's a lot harder than you'd think. They keep popping."

WHAT MIMI COULD MAKE

SNAKE

WORM

SKINNY FISH

CARROT

LITTLE SAUSAGES

WHAT HAPPENED AFTER BREAKFAST

I decided not to say anything about Mimi's outfit. I knew exactly why she was wearing it, so what was there to talk about? I was only hoping it was going to work.

Mimi and I practiced balloon animals for a while, but she was right: it was hard. In the end we were not much better than when we started, but it was fun!

WHAT HAPPENED ON MOVING DAY

On the way over to Mrs. Luther's house I started to get kind of nervous. Mimi seemed totally fine and happy. I was wishing I could feel like that too. The minute I saw Lily I knew that Mimi was going to be sad. Lily was wearing a tutu just like before, but instead of it being pink it was bright blue.

Lily's mom was standing next to Lily. *"Bonjour, les filles,"* she said. It was cool that she was speaking French to us even though I didn't really know exactly what she was saying. I don't know French so I just said, "Hi, Yvonne. Hi, Lily." Lily's mom was one of those moms who wants you to call her by her first name. "Grace! Grace! Grace!" Lily grabbed my hand and started jumping up and down. "Guess what my new favorite color is? Guess?" I know that little kids like it when you give them wrong answers. So I said, "Yellow? Green? Purple?" even though I knew the answer was for sure going to be blue.

"It's blue! See!" shouted Lily. She held out her skirt and twirled so we could both see. I was glad that she wasn't just talking to me. "And you love pink," she said, pointing at Mimi. "I liked pink five weeks ago, but now I love blue." "She changes almost every day," said Yvonne. Mimi looked uncomfortable, like maybe she wanted to run away or throw up, but she just fidgeted and looked down. I was glad she was staying.

WHAT I WAS HAPPY ABOUT

1. Even though they pretty much all looked the same, Lily really liked the balloon creations.

2. She did not ask Mimi to be a troll or any other kind of disgusting creature.

3. Yvonne made us sandwiches and lemonade so we could have a picnic outside.

4. Mimi had a great activity suggestion that took up a huge part of the time, plus it was lots of fun.

The only bad thing was that Lily didn't spend any time talking to Mimi. She wasn't mean to Mimi, but she wasn't super friendly to her either.

WHAT WAS HARD TO BELIEVE

When it turned two o'clock, I couldn't believe it was already time to be done. Yvonne came over to thank us for watching Lily, and it was a good thing that she was taking Lily somewhere fun, or she would have for sure been upset about us leaving. I know this because as soon as Lily saw her mom walking over she said, "I don't want them to go. Can Grace stay for a sleepover?" Mimi was probably not so happy that Lily had said only my name, but she was kind and generous and didn't say one word about it.

YOU CAN'T SLEEP OVER. I HAVE TO GO TO A BIRTHDAY PARTY.

THE OTHER THING THAT WAS HARD TO BELIEVE

Yvonne gave us each ten dollars! That was a lot of money. Mom was going to be freaked out! Hopefully she wasn't going to make me give it back. Of course we said, "Thank you. Thank you. Thank you." About ten thousand times.

WHAT BEING A MOTHER'S HELPER CAN DO TO YOU

Both Mimi and I were super tired so we decided to just go home instead of hanging out.

I guess even though it seemed pretty fun, having a job really is hard work.

WHAT YOU HAVE TO DO

Sometimes when you get something unexpected you have to touch it over and over again to help your brain believe that it is real. It's almost like it has magic powers, because each time you look at it and touch it, it makes you feel happy all over again. After a while Mom said I had to put the ten dollars away before it got ripped. She was right—it was probably a good thing to do. Somehow this ten dollars felt special and different from the ten dollars Grandma gave me for my birthday. I didn't want to get them mixed up, so I put the new ten dollars in my jewelry case instead of in my money box.

MY MONEY BOX THAT USED TO BE A SHOE BOX.

WHAT I AM GLAD ABOUT

I'm glad that no one gets to see my comics except me, because now I was feeling a little bad about making Lily into the Terrible Tutu.

WHAT I ALMOST FORGOT

Just as I was about to fall asleep I remembered that I forgot to flash my lights for Mimi. I was super tired, but I got out of bed anyway. It's like having to go to the bathroom in the middle of the night. Your body wants to stay in the cozy bed, but your brain knows you really need to get up, and so you make yourself do it. As soon as my hand reached the light switch Mimi flicked her lights at me too. That made it totally worth it.

CURSIVE DAY

I was happy about school today, and feeling pretty good about going. Today we were going to finish off learning all of the capital cursive letters. On Friday, Miss Lois had said that if we practiced enough we might be able to have our writing look as good as the writing that is on fancy invitations. Mostly everyone was excited about that.

LILY ON A MONDAY

While I was waiting outside for Mimi I saw Lily getting into the car with her mom. She saw me watching her and shouted, *"Au revoir,* Grace! I'm going to school!" "Me too!" I answered back. From far away like this she was cute. Of course she wasn't going to real school.

MIMI

I was glad to see that Mimi was not wearing an all-blue outfit. She actually looked pretty normal, except for a big flower in her hair. It didn't look bad—it just wasn't a usual Mimi thing.

TWO BY TWO

We started walking and by the time we got to the corner Sammy and Max were walking with us too. Sammy seemed much happier than he had been on Friday. Max was full of questions about the new French family, but I had to answer them all because Mimi was not being her normal chatty self. I don't think he was finding what I was saying very interesting. As soon as we got to the playground, he waved at us all and ran off.

"Boys are so rude," said Mimi. She crossed her arms and made a grumpy face. Sammy was still standing next to us, so I felt like I had to say something. "Well, maybe not all boys." "Thanks," said Sammy. He shrugged his shoulders and walked on without us. "Mimi, what's going on? Are you mad at Max or Sammy?" Mimi seemed nervous. "No, I'm fine. It's okay." And then before I could ask her anything more the bell rang and we had to run so we wouldn't be late.

THE GIGGLY GIRLS

Normally at school Mimi and I don't do too much with the Giggly Girls. We call them that because they are always telling secrets and laughing. I don't know what they think is so funny, but after a while just being near them is kind of annoying.

After we had been in class for about an hour, I could tell that Mimi was being interested in them. She asked Bethany if she could borrow her eraser, and then when she gave it back she whispered something that made her laugh. Bethany is the leader of the Giggly Girls. She lives in a house full of sisters. My friend Jordan once said that someone told her that all the sisters were gigglers. I don't know if it's true, but if it is, being in their house would for sure make me crazy.

THE OTHER BIG REASON WHY I KNOW THAT MIMI IS INTERESTED IN THE GIGGLY GIRLS

Sometimes even if you notice something unusual, you might not understand why the unusual thing is there until later on. This is exactly what happened with Mimi's hair flower. Looking at her, and then at all the Giggly Girls, I suddenly knew why she had the flower in her hair.

MIMI   BETHANY   SARAH   ISABELLA

It was shocking! It was surprising! It was unbelievable! Mimi was trying to look just like them.

Now I knew exactly why Mimi was being so quiet and not friendly with Max and Sammy. The Giggly Girls never talk to boys.

WHAT I WAS GLAD ABOUT

I was glad that Miss Lois was teaching us something interesting, because just trying to think about why Mimi was being weird was making my head hurt. I decided not to pay attention to her, and instead I used all my energy to make the best capital script D that I had ever made in my entire life. It was pretty good!

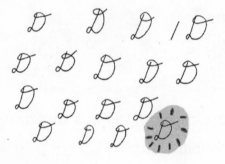

When I looked up, Mimi had taken the flower out of her hair and was smiling at me. A normal me would have been super happy about that, but this new suspicious-of-Mimi me was not 100 percent sure that Mimi wasn't going to suddenly change and be weird again by lunchtime.

WHAT HAPPENED AT LUNCHTIME

Nothing new. Mimi was completely normal. I was surprised, and now it seemed safe to be happy about it. Mimi even waved to Max when he ran by with Sammy. We did the monkey bars, played box ball, and went on the swings—all my favorite things.

WHAT MIMI DID NOT EVEN MENTION ONCE

1. The Fairy Girls
2. The Giggly Girls

WHAT IS HARD TO HIDE

If you have a friend who is acting strange it is hard to say, "Hey, how come you are acting so strange?" For some reason it is easier to ask about happy and sad than it is about weird.

That is why, even though Mimi and I are best friends, I asked, "Is everything okay?" instead of "Why are you acting so strange?" Mimi looked down at the ground for a second and then she said, "Do you think my new sister is going to like me? What if she's all girly and I'm not? What if she wants me to be giggly or play fairy games or something I haven't even thought of yet? You don't have to worry. Little girls like you. Like Lily—she totally loves you, and you're not even her sister."

This was a big problem to solve during lunchtime, especially a lunchtime that was probably going to be ending in about three minutes. "Oh, Mimi," I said, and I gave her a hug. A hug almost always helps a sad person feel even just a little bit better, plus I couldn't think of anything else to say.

I was happy and sad at the same time— happy to know that Mimi was the same old

Mimi, but sad to think that maybe she thought being the same old Mimi wasn't going to be good enough.

WHAT HAPPENED NEXT

Of course as soon as I knew about Mimi being sad, my empathy power started working super fast. This made regular school learning much harder.

1. It was not easy to make up math word problems while my brain was thinking about Mimi.

2. It was not easy to study the continents and the oceans of the world while my brain was thinking about Mimi.

By the time school ended I was as unhappy as she was.

THE ONE THING I WAS PRETTY MUCH KNOWING

Even if Mimi's sister turned out to be super pink, doll loving, and girly, she was for sure still going to love Mimi, because Mimi is fun and great and fantastic! And after being with her, and doing stuff with her, the new sister would not be able to help it—she would end up loving Mimi just as much as I do. And then, as soon as I thought that, I got an idea about exactly what to do.

MY GOOD LUCK SIGN

I didn't tell Mimi about my plan as we walked home. I wanted to, but the part of me that wanted it to be a good surprise for her was bigger than the part of me that wanted to tell her, so I kept it secret. Instead I tried to cheer her up by talking about other stuff.

The biggest thing we talked about was Gary the Great. He is a magician that is going to come to our school and do tricks. The boys are all hoping he is going to saw someone in half. Mostly they would like him to saw Mrs. Hopkins in half. She is one of the bossy ladies who stand outside and make sure everyone lines up properly when the bell rings. She yells a lot, and usually it's at the boys.

Right when we were talking about Gary the Great, we passed a poster about him that was taped to a light pole. Mimi wanted to stop and look at it so we would be able to recognize him if we saw him around town. We were both wondering if he did magic tricks in his real life, like maybe at the grocery store. A good magician could probably trick people all the time and the people wouldn't even know about it. He could pay the grocery person, and then when they weren't looking, use his tricks to sneak the money back into his pocket—stuff like that. Mimi said, "If we see him in the grocery store we should one hundred percent spy on him." Just thinking about that was kind of exciting.

While Mimi was putting his face into her memory, I thought some more about my plan. And then for no real reason I looked down at my foot, and there by my pinky toe was an almost perfectly round white stone. Of course I had to pick it up. "Ewww," said Mimi. "What if a dog peed on it?" But she was too late. It was already in my pocket.

WHAT MIMI WANTED

"Do you want to come over?" asked Mimi. "We could work on the room." This was a hard question to answer. I wanted to go over and keep her company, but also I wanted to get home and start on my big plan. To keep her happy and not suspicious I said, "Okay, but I can only come over for an hour."

WHAT TOOK US AN HOUR

It took one whole hour to decide which wall was going to be the one we were going to paint pink. This was mostly because Mimi kept changing her mind. In the end I think she picked the right one.

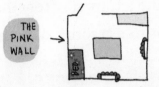

MIMI PICKED THIS ONE BECAUSE IT WAS THE BIGGEST PIECE OF WALL WITHOUT ANYTHING ELSE ON IT—NO WINDOWS OR CLOSET.

WHAT I DID AS SOON AS I GOT HOME

I started my big plan. I was going to make a shadow show in my window for Lily and Mimi to watch together from Mimi's window. I even had a name for the show. In my best script writing I wrote the title out on a black piece of paper. It looked great. The only hard part was cutting out all the white parts so just the black heart and words were showing.

It was lucky that we were learning cursive, because if you want to cut out words and have all the letters stay together the only way to do it is to use script writing.

WORD
CAN STAY TOGETHER
IF YOU LIFT THE PIECE
OF PAPER UP

WORD
WILL NOT
STAY TOGETHER.

WHAT I DON'T KNOW THE WORDS FOR

There is probably a name for the kind of plan that was in my brain. It was the kind of plan where the people watching the show (Mimi and Lily) weren't going to know that the watching of the show was only one part of the plan. Them being together and doing things together was the other part of the plan. Lily was definitely going to be liking Mimi once she spent time with her and found out how fun and special she was.

HOW THIS CAN HAPPEN

Lily needs to love Mimi like she loves me. And if Lily is around Mimi, and does stuff with Mimi, she won't be able to help herself. Before long she will love Mimi as much as she loves me.

PART ONE OF THE PLAN

It was kind of hard to decide which part of the plan should be part one. When you are at the beginning of something you can start from all sorts of places. I decided that my part one should start with Augustine Dupre. Lucky for me, it wasn't dinnertime yet so I was still allowed to go downstairs and visit her.

HEAD ON NICE PILLOW

When I walked in Crinkles was lying on the sofa like usual. "I think he's scared of Lily," said Augustine Dupre. "He's over here all the time." I didn't say it, but if I were a cat, I'd pick Augustine Dupre instead of Lily too. I didn't want to waste time talking about Crinkles, so I told her about my plan right away. And just like I was hoping, she said she would talk to Lily's mom and set it up so Lily could go to Mimi's house.

PART TWO OF THE PLAN

It's not always easy to explain big ideas to grownups. Mimi's mom is super nice, but what I had to ask her about was not something she normally would say yes to. I was going to ask her if we could break one of her big house rules—the rule of no food in Mimi's bedroom—and I was nervous about that.

The only good thing about part two of the plan was that I had to wait until tomorrow to do it, because Mom was calling me down for dinner.

PART THREE OF THE PLAN

After dinner I started part three of the plan. Sometimes you have to be able to skip around in a plan and not be worried about the number order so much. I was happy about that, because the invitation was really fun to do.

WHAT IS HARD TO HIDE

1. A really good mood.

GOOD MOOD ANALOGY

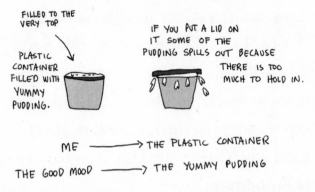

FILLED TO THE VERY TOP

PLASTIC CONTAINER FILLED WITH YUMMY PUDDING.

IF YOU PUT A LID ON IT SOME OF THE PUDDING SPILLS OUT BECAUSE THERE IS TOO MUCH TO HOLD IN.

ME ———→ THE PLASTIC CONTAINER

THE GOOD MOOD ———→ THE YUMMY PUDDING

WHO IT IS HARD TO HIDE IT FROM

1. Your parents.

At breakfast both Mom and Dad said, "Why are you in such a good mood today?" Lucky for me, I had already thought of an answer. "We are having this really cool magician come to the school today. His name is Gary the Great and he does all sort of cool tricks. He might even saw someone in half."

Whenever there is something new and interesting at school Mom and Dad always say the same thing. It's usually something like, "I wish I could go to school. We never had things like that when we were kids. All we did was work." And then they look at each other and shake their heads. I'm glad I wasn't a kid when they were kids. It must have been really boring.

2. Your best friend.

I tried to not seem excited and happy when I saw Mimi, but she could tell I was hiding something. "Why are you smiling?" she asked. I tried to use the same Gary the Great excuse, but right when I was explaining how fun I thought he was going to be, Sammy walked up. "Hey, are you guys talking about Gary the Great?" "Yeah." I said. "I hope he's good. I like magic tricks." Sammy did not seem excited. "He's not a magician," said Sammy. "He's a math-gician. He does tricks with numbers. Boring math stuff." "Ohhh," said Mimi.

I looked at Sammy. "It's true," he said. I didn't want to, but I believed him. Now school was not going to be as fun as I thought it was. I should have known the school would try to sneak some lessons into something that was supposed to be all fun.

Now I was not as happy as before. My really good mood was now only a medium good mood.

NOW I DON'T HAVE TO PRETEND TO NOT BE SUPER HAPPY.

GARY THE GREAT

SURPRISE! Gary the Great **was** great! He did a lot of math tricks that were math problems, but they had stories and real magic tricks mixed in so it was fun. I thought he would just do lots of adding and subtracting, but it wasn't like that at all.

My favorite trick was when he made a recipe of all sorts of crazy things. Before the trick started he asked the audience for a number.

Then Gary the Great put that many things into a bucket to make the recipe. At the end of the trick, the bucket was empty except for a super-long stuffed snake. He even used the word "TA-DA!" Which is one of my favorite things to say that I had mostly forgotten about.

He was so good that only a couple of kids complained that he had not sawed anyone in half. They were probably kids that did not like math or Mrs. Hopkins.

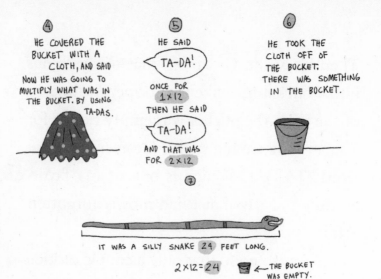

④ HE COVERED THE BUCKET WITH A CLOTH, AND SAID NOW HE WAS GOING TO MULTIPLY WHAT WAS IN THE BUCKET, BY USING TA-DAS.

⑤ HE SAID TA-DA! ONCE FOR 1×12 THEN HE SAID TA-DA! AND THAT WAS FOR 2×12

⑥ HE TOOK THE CLOTH OFF OF THE BUCKET. THERE WAS SOMETHING IN THE BUCKET.

⑦

IT WAS A SILLY SNAKE 24 FEET LONG.

2×12=24 ← THE BUCKET WAS EMPTY.

HOW MISS LOIS SURPRISED US

She said we had to write a secret note in cursive writing and pass it to the person who was sitting to the right of us. This was the first on-purpose note passing we had ever done. Miss Lois said that we had to be sure that the note was something nice, and not anything that would hurt someone's feelings. She said, "I don't want anyone writing *Your sneakers smell like old cheese.*" This made us all smile and joke around.

Sammy was sitting on my right, which was lucky for me because I had the perfect thing to write for him.

> *I found a Gary the Great stone for you.*

Sunni gave me her note. Her script writing was excellent, which was no surprise. It was nice that she wrote me a compliment.

> *I think you are very nice and I like your hair.*

WHAT HAPPENED AFTER SCHOOL

Sammy wanted to walk home with Mimi and me so he could get his stone. It was nice

to have Mimi being normal again and being friendly to Sammy. As soon as we got to
my front yard Lily came running over. "Hi,
Grace." She grabbed my hand like we were
best friends. She said hi to Mimi too, but she
did not say her name. I was sorry about that.
Mom says you should use a person's name
when you meet them, because it makes them
feel more special. She is right about that, because it really does.

HERE IS AN EXAMPLE:

I introduced Lily to Sammy, but she said
she'd already met him when he'd gotten his

jar of rocks. They kind of just smiled at each other and didn't say anything.

Today Lily was wearing a yellow tutu. I was suddenly getting the feeling that she probably had a big collection of tutus in all sorts of colors.

WHAT HAPPENED NEXT

Lily's mom, Yvonne, came over to drag Lily back to their house. This was a big relief, because I had a lot to do for the show, plus I had all my regular homework too. I did not have any extra time left over to be playing with Lily. Everyone else went home too except for Sammy. He waited on the front steps while I ran in to get his rock.

I HOPE IT'S A GOOD STONE.

WHAT I WOULD NEVER SAY

"Wow! This is a great rock—thank you." But coming out of Sammy's mouth it sounded perfectly normal. and it made me happy.

WHAT I SAW THAT WAS UNUSUAL

After Sammy left, I saw Mimi standing in Mrs. Luther's driveway. She was talking to Yvonne and Lily. Normally I would have run over there to see what was going on, but instead I made myself sneak over to Mimi's house to talk to her mom about part two.

WHAT FEELS GOOD

Mimi's mom is so nice. Now that I did my talking to her, it's hard to even remember why I was thinking I was going to be nervous about it. She said yes to part two of the plan. And the best part of all was that Mimi didn't even see me asking her. The show was still going to be a surprise, and I was happy about that! It made it even more exciting.

I was back in my yard when Mimi walked back from Mrs. Luther's. "I was giving Yvonne my old hula hoops for Lily," said Mimi. "Good idea," I said.

Mimi couldn't talk anymore because her mom called her in for dinner. As I was waving goodbye it looked like her mom winked at me, or maybe a bug flew in her eye. It was hard to tell 100 percent, but I was pretty sure it was a wink.

PART FOUR OF THE PLAN

Part four of the plan is the making part of the plan, and it was probably going to take a long time to finish it. The bad thing about a big plan is that when you are doing the thinking part of the plan, everything is very exciting and the plan seems like it will be fast and easy to finish. But when you really start working on it, that's when you suddenly know that you were wrong and that the doing part isn't going to be so fast and easy after all.

HOW TO MAKE A SHADOW PUPPET

A. DRAW PICTURE

It's best to draw on black paper with a white crayon. That way you can see your line better.

B. CUT OUT PICTURE

You can use scissors.

PART FIVE OF THE PLAN

Ask Mom to help.

Mom is going to do all the cutting parts and I am going to do the drawing part. Now, with her helping, it is not going to take so long. Mom said she was happy to be helping. She was especially happy after I told her that I really got the idea from something she did for me.

WHAT MOM DID TO HELP ME AT MY FIRST SLEEPOVER AT MIMI'S HOUSE

Even though Mimi lives just next door, when I was little I was scared to sleep in a bed that was not in my room. I really wanted to sleep over at Mimi's, but I did not want to miss Mom saying good night to me. Mom told me she had a surprise for me, and that when it was bedtime at Mimi's house she wanted me to look out Mimi's window and watch my bedroom window.

This is the show she made me. It started with window one and ended with window three.

WINDOW ONE

THIS IS A LITTLE
STICK TO HOLD
THE WORD UP

WINDOW TWO

WINDOW THREE

MOM LEFT THE LIGHT
ON IN MY ROOM ALL
NIGHT SO I COULD
LOOK AT THE STAR WINDOW
WHENEVER I WANTED.

Mom always used to call me her little star, so this was a perfect little show for me to see.

THIS IS HOW MOM DID IT

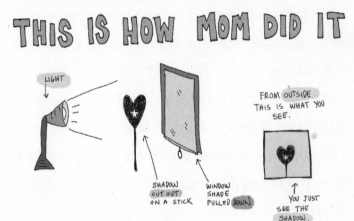

LIGHT

FROM OUTSIDE
THIS IS WHAT YOU
SEE.

SHADOW
CUT OUT
ON A STICK

WINDOW
SHADE
PULLED DOWN

YOU JUST
SEE THE
SHADOW.

WHAT LILY WAS WEARING ON THURSDAY

Lily was wearing a green tutu. She didn't see me watching her from the front yard, so I shouted her name and waved. This was new for me. NO hiding.

Mimi came out a few minutes later and we had a nice walk to school—just the two of us.

THE BIG THING THAT HAPPENED AT SCHOOL

The only interesting thing that happened at school today was that Miss Lois gave Owen 1 a gold star on his folder for going the whole entire day without playing with the Velcro on his shoes. This probably made it a big special day for him, but for the rest of us it was just like any other day except without the ripping noise.

WHAT HAPPENED AFTER SCHOOL

I told Mimi I wanted to get home to do my homework, but really I needed to get working on the show. Mimi said she was going to do some more sister-room designing. I could tell that she was still really nervous about making the right choices, because now she was thinking about having the room be totally decorated with teddy bears. Yesterday she said it was going to be bunnies, or ducks, or balloons. She was having a hard time deciding on anything. I was having the feeling that the sister-room project was not turning out to be as much fun as she thought it would be.

Mimi is filled with worry.

WHAT HAPPENED WHILE MOM AND I WERE WORKING

Augustine Dupre came upstairs to tell me that everything was set for Friday night. She said Yvonne was going to bring Lily over at seven-thirty. I could tell that she would have liked to watch the show too, but it was a special performance for Mimi and Lily only.

WHAT IS NICE

It's nice to go to sleep thinking that you are ready for something you have been working on. I knew that Mom and I were going to finish on time, and in my head everything was going to work out perfectly. It had to.

WHAT HAPPENS WHEN YOU ARE SUPER EXCITED

You get dressed, eat your breakfast, and are completely ready for school by 7:14 a.m.

WHAT IS NOT SO GOOD

Being ready for school over an hour early and having nothing else to do but wait, because school doesn't start until 8:45. Mom made me wait until it was 8:00 before she let me go over to Mimi's house to give her the invitation. Once I got there I had to wait some more, because Mimi was still upstairs getting dressed.

WHAT MIMI SAID WHEN SHE SAW THE INVITATION

"OH MY GOSH, GRACE! WHAT IS THIS? IT'S FOR ME? I CAN'T BELIEVE IT. TELL

ME!!!! TELL ME!!" And then she started to do little bounces up and down like she always does when she gets super excited. If you spent four days making your best friend a special show, this is the exact kind of perfect way you would want her to act when she found out about it.

WHAT I TOLD MIMI ABOUT THE SHOW

Nothing. I said, "Mimi, I can't tell you anything. It's a surprise."

WHAT WAS LONG

When you are waiting for something that is going to happen at the end of a day, the whole part of the day that is in front of the end part can seem like it is taking forever. School felt like it was never going to end. Even though some good things happened, it still seemed to go by super slow.

THE GOOD THINGS THAT HAPPENED

1. We watched a video of an elephant that could write the words *love* and *hope* in cursive. Miss Lois told us it was a boy elephant, and if a boy elephant could write in cursive, then a boy human should be able to do it too. Everyone thought this was pretty funny, even the boys.

2. Grace F.'s birthday's on Saturday, so we all got to have blueberry muffins at snack-time. Cupcakes would have been better, but Mr. Harris is trying to get all the kids not to eat so many sweets, so Grace F.'s mom had to make muffins instead.

NO ICING

ICING

MUFFIN   CUPCAKE

3. Because the muffins took so long to eat, Miss Lois canceled our spelling test for today and said we would have it on Monday instead.

NO SPELLING THOUGHTS IN HERE.

4. Brian Aber's dad came to the class to show us his banjo. He played two songs and was really good. He said he did not know how to the play the guitar, which was a surprise because they both kind of look the same. I was wishing he would stay longer so we wouldn't have to do math, but Miss Lois wouldn't let him play any more songs or answer any more questions, so he had to leave. She really is the boss of the classroom, even when there is a dad there.

FINALLY

When the bell rang Mimi and I walked straight home. She was going to clean up her room and I was going to finish up the show with Mom.

WHAT MOM SAID

Right before Lily came over Mom told me that no matter what happened she was very proud of me. This was a nice thing to hear, and I was hoping she was going to remember this happiness the next time she was thinking about getting mad at me for some reason.

Before, when I was still getting stuff ready I was not one bit worried about anything, but now the waiting-for-it-to-start part was making me nervous. It was taking forever for Augustine Dupre to bring Lily over. Suddenly my brain was thinking of all the things that could go wrong, and it was not easy to get it to stop.

It was a huge relief when Lily said, "Grace! Grace! I'm here. You can stop waiting."

THE START

Lily gave me a big hug and for once I was happy about that. Like always, she was wearing a tutu. This time it was a purple one. "It's the best twirler of all my tutus," said Lily, and then she did a twirl to show me. "You're right," I said. "It is a good one." And then after about five more twirls we started our walk over to Mimi's.

LILY
TWIRLING

It was just starting to get dark, which is the perfect kind of light for a shadow show.

Mimi was excited too, and I knew that, because instead of waiting for us inside, she met us in her front yard. It was not easy to try to pretend like I was not nervous. All three of us walked up to Mimi's room.

Right when we got to Mimi's room I said, "Remember that cool clapping song game we used to do at school?" It was one of those games where you say a rhyme and clap your hands together at the same time. Mimi and I used to do it all the time last year, and I was hoping like crazy that she was going to remember it. "The one with the made-up words?" asked Mimi. Yay! She remembered. "Yes, that's it," I said. "When you see the hands, teach it to Lily." Of course Mimi didn't know what I was talking about, but I was hoping she would understand when she saw the show.

I was glad to see that her room was super cleaned up and organized. Mimi had two little chairs sitting in front of the bedroom window. I looked across at my window and suddenly my ears started to get hot. This only happens to me when I get nervous or when I am embarrassed. It is not a good feeling.

I couldn't wait around. I had to leave. "Mimi, don't open these until you see the signs in the window." I handed her four brown bags with big numbers on them, and then ran down the stairs. "Be careful," shouted Mimi's mom, but I was too filled with nervousness to slow down.

THE FOUR BAGS

THE UNFORTUNATE PART OF THE PLAN

The only bad thing about my plan was that there was no way for me to know what was going on in Mimi's room. I wouldn't be able to tell if Mimi and Lily were having a fun time or a terrible time. Once I started the show I would just have to keep going until the end, hoping everything would work out.

THE SHOW

This is what Mimi and Lily saw looking out Mimi's window over to my window.

It was fun to do the dolphin swimming up and down. Dolphins are one of my favorite animals, so I worked extra hard to make it look good.

When Mimi opened this bag there was a note inside that said, "Tell Lily about how your dad pretends to be a dolphin and how it feels to ride on his back, because Lily likes mermaids and a dolphin swimming probably feels just like a mermaid swimming."

Now it was time for Lily's favorite thing to do: twirling.

This one was really easy to do because I just had to spin the princess puppet around and it was going to look super good.

Of course Lily couldn't read this, but I was pretty sure that as soon as Mimi told her what it said Lily would twirl. Lily was an expert twirler and it was one of her favorite things to do.

Then I put up the Mimi twirl sign, and in my imagination I could just see them both twirling around Mimi's room like crazy. Even though I couldn't see them, just thinking about it made me smile and feel happy.

This is the one I had to ask Mimi's mom about, because in bag number two were some jelly doughnuts and lemonade juice boxes. Lily was for sure going to make a mess with the doughnuts, so it was nice that Mimi's mom was ready for that and was not going to be getting mad about a food mess in Mimi's room.

I had to wait for a while now and do nothing. This was the hard part, trying to imagine how long it would take them to finish the doughnuts and lemonade. When enough time had passed I started with the show again.

I was sure hoping that Mimi was going to

remember what we had talked about in her
bedroom.

I said the clapping poem in my head as I
moved the shadow hands back and forth.

Now it was time for bag number three.
This was one of my favorites.

Inside bag three were two dishtowels, two
clothes pegs, and some yellow tape that Mom

said I could have. The note inside said for Mimi to make two capes, one for her and one for Lily, and then wind up her favorite music box and jump on the bed until the music stopped. I didn't ask Mimi's mom about this one, which was probably good because I was pretty sure she would have said no. Mimi's mom is not a you-can-jump-on-the-bed kind of mom. I put these drawings inside the bag so Mimi could better understand what she was supposed to do.

Mimi is excellent at making stuff and super good at sewing, so I bet she didn't have any trouble at all. I really wish I could have been seeing this part. I made a little superhero guy to fly around in the window. Mostly so I would have something to do while they were bouncing up and down.

Bag four was filled with light sticks, the kind you crack and then they glow in the dark. I didn't need to put in any instructions because everyone knows what to do with those. As soon as I saw Mimi and Lily waving them around I put up my end of show sign.

WHAT I DID WHEN I SAW THE LIGHT STICKS

I smiled super big, jumped up and down, and then fell on my back onto my bed with my arms out like a starfish.

I was filled with relief. Mom kept peeking around the corner at me, so I finally got up. I think she was probably dying to know how it had worked out. I was dying to know too.

WHAT HAPPENED AT MIMI'S HOUSE

As soon as I got to the door of Mimi's house, Mimi's mom put her fingers up to her lips and made the shush sound. This was a good thing to do because if she hadn't I would have for sure shouted Mimi's name. If you are excited, being loud is easier than being quiet. I crept upstairs quietly and went into Mimi's room.

WHAT I SAW

Lily sleeping on Mimi's bed.

WHAT I FELT

Mimi's arms around me giving me the biggest hug ever.

WHAT MIMI SAID

Mimi said the show was amazing, awesome, wonderful, and fantastic, but the number one best thing she said was "I think Lily likes me now."

WHAT HAPPENED NEXT

Lily's mom came to get her, but since Lily was asleep Mimi asked if she could leave her sleeping. I said I would stay over too, and then we both did our big puppy dog eyes so she would have to say yes. At first it looked like she might say no, but then she changed her mind. I thought Mimi would scream with joy, but she did a good job of holding in her excitement and happiness quietly. She didn't want to wake up Lily and have her go home.

I ran back home to ask Mom and get my sleepover stuff and then Mimi and I put out our sleeping bags next to each other on the floor. We both really wanted to talk about the night. "Tell me everything," I said. I was listening, and even though I was super interested, I couldn't help it—I fell asleep almost as soon as Mimi started talking.

THE ONE TIME WHEN HAVING TO GET UP IN THE MIDDLE OF THE NIGHT WAS A GOOD THING

In the middle of the night I had to get up to go to the bathroom, and just by accident looked out Mimi's window. This is what I saw on my window.

It was just like the MOM-WOW, but for me.

I have the best mom in the world! And for sure I was going to try to remember this for the next time I was not feeling happy with her.

WHAT HAPPENED THE NEXT DAY

The first thing that happened that surprised me and Mimi both was that Lily woke up at six-thirty. This is extra early for a Saturday. At first she was pretty surprised that she was still in Mimi's room, but then she got super excited because she had done her first sleepover like a big girl.

I thought Mimi's mom might be mad because we were up so early, and Lily was making a lot of noise bouncing on the bed. But she wasn't grumpy at all. She said it was good practice for when they got their own little girl. As soon as she said that Lily said, "You're getting a little girl? Is she going to sleep in

Mimi's bed too?" Mimi's mom covered her mouth, but it was too late. She had told the secret.

WHAT WE ALL KNEW

Lily was not going to be a very good secret keeper.

HOW LILY HELPED MIMI

Lily was super excited that Mimi was going to get a new sister. She was full of questions. Mostly she wanted to know where the new sister was going to sleep. Mimi took her to the new-sister room. It was not looking very fabulous because nothing was decorated yet. "What color are you going to make it?" asked Lily. "One quarter pink," said Mimi. Lily looked around and said, "Are the nickels and the pennies going to be all the other colors?"

And that is how Mimi suddenly knew what the perfect room decoration should be: white walls with big round circles in all the colors of the rainbow.

WALL WITH
COLORED
↓ CIRCLES ON
IT.

WHAT WE WERE RIGHT ABOUT

After breakfast Mimi and I walked Lily home. Sammy was standing at Mrs. Luther's house. As soon as Lily saw him she said, "Guess what? Guess what Mimi's getting?" Lily was not even a little bit of a secret keeper.

What Was a Surprise Times Three

Lily was waiting for Sammy to make a guess but he wasn't saying anything so she gave him a hint. "It's something super cute and fun!" Sammy looked nervous. "Give up?" asked Lily. She didn't wait for him to answer. "A sister! Mimi's getting a little sister. And I'm helping her learn all about little girls." Sammy looked relieved. "Wow, that's great. I thought you were going to say a cat." How Sammy could forget that Mimi was allergic to cats is another of those big Sammy mysteries.

And then without even asking a question about it or anything more, Sammy said, "Okay. Are you ready to look for rocks?" "You bet!" said Lily. "Bye, Grace. Bye, Mimi. I have to go. I'm getting a rock collection."

Mimi and I both looked at each other with

our mouths open, because that is what you have to do when you are fully surprised.

And then Mimi said something that was perfect, because sometimes if your world is full of changes, it's nice to do something regular and familiar.

We walked to Mimi's without saying a word, but even though my mouth was quiet, my brain was doing lots of thinking. It was thinking about Sammy and Lily knowing each other, Sammy and Lily liking each other, and Lily finally liking Mimi. Then when I turned around for one last look, it started thinking something new.

And for the first time ever I thought, *Mimi's new sister is probably going to be a lot of fun for me too.* This was a good thought to have, because as soon as we walked into Mimi's house Mimi's mom came over and gave us both a big hug. "Good news!" she said. "We passed the parent test! Now all we have is the house test." "Oh my gosh!" said Mimi. "I've got to clean my room!" She was right. Her room was a disaster again, and even though my stomach wanted the banana bread, I made my brain win. Mimi needed my help, and sometimes there are things more important than food.

WHY ARE COMICS SUDDENLY SO POPULAR?
DO I KNOW TOO MUCH ABOUT SAMMY?
WHY IS BOY WORLD SO STRANGE?
IS MIMI GOING TO BE UPSET FOR THE REST OF HER LIFE?
WHY IS AUGUSTINE DUPRE WEARING A SUPER CAPE?